ROBERT IRWIN
DINOSAUR HUNTER

ARMOURED DEFENCE

3

SCAN THE QR CODE ON THE BACK COVER
TO UNLOCK A SPECIAL MESSAGE FROM
ROBERT IRWIN

Other books in the
Robert Irwin, Dinosaur Hunter series:

The Discovery

Ambush at Cisco Swamp

The Dinosaur Feather

ARMOURED DEFENCE

WRITTEN BY JACK WELLS

RANDOM HOUSE AUSTRALIA

A Random House book
Published by Random House Australia Pty Ltd
Level 3, 100 Pacific Highway, North Sydney NSW 2060
www.randomhouse.com.au

First published by Random House Australia in 2013

Addresses for companies within the Random House Group can be found at
www.randomhouse.com.au/offices

National Library of Australia
Cataloguing-in-Publication Entry

Author: Irwin, Robert, 2003–
Title: Armoured Defence / Robert Irwin, Jack Wells.
ISBN: 978 1 74275 091 0 (pbk.)
Series: Robert Irwin dinosaur hunter; 3.
Target Audience: For primary school age children.
Subjects: Dinosaurs – Juvenile fiction.
Other Authors/Contributors: Kunz, Chris.
Dewey Number: A823.4

Cover and internal illustrations by Lachlan Creagh
Cover and internal design by Christabella Designs
Typeset by Midland Typesetters, Australia
Printed in Australia by Griffin Press, an accredited ISO AS/NZS
14001:2004 Environmental Management System printer

Random House Australia uses papers that are natural, renewable and
recyclable products and made from wood grown in sustainable forests.
The logging and manufacturing processes are expected to conform to the
environmental regulations of the country of origin.

CHAPTER ONE

'Awesome! We're 26 metres off the ground up here!' Robert shouted out excitedly, taking in the view. 'Look, Riley, those people down there are smaller than ants. They're like microscopic amoeba or something. Amazing!'

Robert's best friend, on the other

hand, was looking a little green around the gills and refused to look down. He kept his eyes very firmly on the horizon. 'Please don't mention how high up we are,' Riley mumbled.

'Twenty-six metres equals about 86 feet. Does that sound better to you?'

Riley considered this for a moment. 'If I think of it as 86 of *my* feet, that doesn't sound so bad.'

Robert chuckled. 'Whatever works for you, buddy.'

Recently, Robert's life had changed quite dramatically after he'd found

a magic fossil that allowed him to travel back to the Age of Dinosaurs. But never in his wildest dreams had he ever considered being able to stand in the mouth of the world's largest T-rex!

Of course, this wasn't a *real* T-rex. It was a huge steel replica of one but, just like the big pineapple in Queensland, this T-rex was bigger than the real thing – four and a half times bigger to be exact. From the statue's open jaw, tourists could survey the famous Canadian Badlands, home of the largest amount of

dinosaur fossil discoveries in the world.

'When I told Uncle Nate you were a dinosaur hunter, he knew you'd love it here in Alberta,' said Riley.

Robert and Riley's families had travelled from Texas, USA to spend a few days at Calgary Zoo, helping to look after some newborn red pandas. Riley's Uncle Nate, who'd lived in Canada since he'd graduated high school, had offered to take the boys on a two-day camping trip in the Canadian Badlands.

'You're gonna love Uncle Nate. He's someone really high up in the Canadian

Army – a general, or maybe even a president or something.'

'I'm not sure you can be a president in the army, can you?' asked Robert.

Riley shrugged. 'Maybe they created a special position for Uncle Nate because he's so good.'

'Maybe,' replied Robert a little doubtfully.

'He's so strong and tough, and he's fought in lots of wars and you don't want to mess with him,' said Riley proudly.

'Mess with who?' said a gruff voice from behind them.

5

'Uncle Nate!' cried Riley, as his uncle lifted him up and spun him around.

'How's my favourite nephew?' Uncle Nate asked, lowering Riley to the ground and holding on to him till he regained his balance. 'I saw your dad down in the car park and he said I'd find you here.'

'I've grown since you saw me last, haven't I?' said Riley, trying to hide his dizziness. It was hard enough being up this high, but getting spun around too?! He wasn't going to look like a wuss in front of his uncle.

'One day you might grow to be as big as your favourite relative,' Uncle Nate said with a laugh. He turned to Robert. 'And you must be the famous Robert Irwin who Riley always talks about.'

Riley frowned. 'I don't always talk about him,' he admonished. 'Sometimes I talk about dirt-biking, and snakes and rugby league and termite mounds . . .'

Uncle Nate interrupted, knowing that when Riley started talking, it was sometimes hard to get him to stop. 'Yes, perhaps Robert's not your only topic of conversation.' He shook Robert's hand. 'Nice to meet you, son.'

'G'day, I've heard a lot about you too, Uncle Nate.'

After days and days of Riley talking about his uncle as this awesomely strong and tough army bloke, it was surprising to Robert that the man in front of him was not the size of a *titanosaur*, or even an *albertosaurus*. Uncle Nate was shorter than average and fit-looking, but not covered in muscles like Robert had imagined. He had a big friendly smile and cropped sandy brown hair.

Uncle Nate chuckled. 'Oh, yeah? It better be good stuff or Riley will be digging the latrines at the camp site.'

Riley looked horrified. 'It was all good stuff, wasn't it, Robert? Tell him. Only good stuff.'

Uncle Nate and Robert laughed as the three of them made their way from the viewing platform and began the hike back down to ground level.

CHAPTER TWO

'Tell Robert about the last time you were in Afghanistan, Uncle Nate,' said Riley as the boys put their seatbelts on.

Uncle Nate manoeuvred the station wagon out of the car park and they hit the open road. 'What do you want to know?'

'Did you fight the enemy and lock them all up?' prompted Riley.

Uncle Nate gave a tired grin. 'It's a bit more complicated than that, buddy. We're over there to help train the national security forces. We're not involved in combat in Afghanistan any more.'

'So you teach the good guys to shoot guns and protect the local people from the bad guys?' Riley's eyes were bugging out of his head.

'Yeah, sure. Something like that. The last trip to Kabul, there was a situation that could've turned deadly . . .'

While Riley hung on his uncle's every word, Robert's mind drifted back to dinosaurs. He took his special fossil out from his pocket, holding it carefully in the palm of his hand. He carried it with him all the time, along with a digital voice recorder, which he used to document the weird and wonderful things he saw on his travels.

The fossil didn't look magical. And most of the time it wasn't. He was never sure when it would transport him back in time, but he figured that since he was

in prime dinosaur territory, it could happen at any moment.

In Texas, after seeing a *deinosuchus* take on an *albertosaurus*, he couldn't keep the time travel a secret any longer. He'd told Riley about the fossil and promised him that, if he could, he'd take his friend along with him the next time. Robert had had no idea if he'd be able to do it, but Riley would never forgive him if he didn't try. He just hoped the fossil didn't send him time-travelling while he was in a moving car!

'. . . it was dangerous and a couple of my soldiers needed bandages and lice treatment, but we got out all right.'

Riley was grinning at his uncle as though he was the best thing since the invention of the dirt bike. 'That's an awesome story, Uncle Nate.'

'Before we get to the camp site, take a look out the window. The badlands are like nowhere else on earth,' said Uncle Nate.

Robert pocketed his fossil and returned to the conversation. 'I've been wondering why this place is called the badlands in the first place.'

Riley sniggered. 'It sounds like the kind of place where cowboys have shootouts.'

'Badlands are areas that are pretty much dry. The rock is soft and has been eroded by the rain and wind, causing some cool geologicial formations to pop up over time,' Uncle Nate explained.

'Like that one?' Robert pointed to a tall rock sculpture, which looked as though it had a mushroom-cup head.

'Exactly. They're called *hoodoos*. The rock on the top is iron stone. It's harder than the rock beneath it, so the pillar has

been worn away. The erosion creates a whole lot of interesting shapes.'

'So the extreme erosion in this area has helped uncover dinosaur fossils?' asked Robert, peering out the car window, quietly hoping to catch sight of an *albertosaurus* skeleton lying by the side of the road. Instead there was only a patch of dry grass.

'That's right. They've found a whole range of dinosaur fossils here. From *triceratops* to *stegosaurs* –'

'*Albertosaurus* and T-rex,' piped up Riley.

'And one of my favourite anklyosaurs, *Euoplocephalus* (you-oh-ploe-seff-ah-luss), has been found here too,' added Robert.

'Is he the guy who looked like an armoured tank?' asked Uncle Nate, overtaking a caravan with a trailer attached. It was peak tourist season and Dinosaur Provincial Park was teeming with holiday-makers.

'That's him, all right. The *euoplocephalus* was covered in protective plates and had a club-like tail. He didn't seem that impressive, but he definitely knew how to stand up for himself.'

Uncle Nate nodded. 'Sounds a bit like me, actually. There are a lot of guys in the army that are bigger and stronger, but sometimes it's the little guys that come up with good defensive tactics.'

Riley scoffed. 'There's nothing interesting about defence. It's all about the attack.' With that, Riley launched himself at Robert, pretending to bite his friend on the neck.

'Ahhhh, get off me.' Robert giggled and tried to defend himself. It was a hard thing to do wearing a seatbelt and not being able to move more than a couple of centimetres away from Riley.

Uncle Nate looked in the rear-view mirror, smiling at the two boys. In his most authoritative voice, he barked, 'Soldiers. The camp site is 15 minutes away. No further attacks on each other until we're out of the car.'

'Yes, sir!' the two boys replied in unison, sitting up straight with eyes ahead.

CHAPTER THREE

The camp site was at the edge of a small lake. More strangely shaped hoodoos in the distance cast interesting shadows over the surrounding grasslands. Riley and Robert were sitting on a couple of foldaway chairs, eating vegemite sandwiches. Uncle Nate had gone off in

search of some cold drinks, leaving the boys to soak up the beautiful and unusual environment.

Riley gobbled up his sandwich first and went to grab the rest of his friend's food. But Robert was too quick. He shoved the rest of the sandwich into his mouth before Riley could get to it. 'Too late, mate,' he said with his mouth full.

'It's never too late for an attack!' With a grin, Riley launched himself again at his friend.

At that moment, Robert felt the

familiar tingle of his fossil. He reached into his pocket, holding the fossil in both hands, a second before Riley landed on him. Before Robert could warn him, the two friends disappeared into the now familiar vortex, falling through time, with Riley still yelling his vegemite war cry. 'Waaaaaa . . .'

'. . . aaaaaahat just happened?!' finished Riley a few moments later, lying breathless on the ground. He looked around him, confused. There were no

longer any foldaway chairs or a tent nearby, or any sign of hoodoos in the distance. Thankfully, though, his best friend was sprawled on the ground next to him.

Riley grabbed his head. 'Man, I feel like someone just chucked me into an angry washing machine.'

Robert stood up warily, glancing at his fossil before pocketing it. 'Riley, mate, you've just time-travelled.'

'Eh?'

'Gone back in time about 70 million years,' Robert explained further.

Riley's eyes widened. 'No way.' But as he glanced around, he realised Robert knew exactly what he was talking about. 'This is epic!'

Robert was all business. He took out his voice recorder and pressed record. 'I've time-travelled, and this time Riley's here with me.'

Riley turned and waved as though the voice recorder was a video recorder.

Robert rolled his eyes good-naturedly. 'I suspect we may have travelled back to the Cretaceous period again, probably still in Alberta.'

Riley whipped around. 'You mean there are *albertosauruses* here?' All of a sudden he wasn't feeling so thrilled to have time-travelled.

Robert nodded. 'Remember that they've found over 35 types of dinosaur fossils in this area, and that might just be a small portion of the animals that roamed these parts.'

'Okay, but tell me there were more herbivores than carnivores here. Please?'

Robert shrugged. 'Half and half. What's interesting is that the herbivores from this era were heavily armoured.'

'To protect themselves from lots of ferocious meat-eaters?' suggested Riley nervously.

Robert nodded.

'Well then, I think it might be time to go back. We don't want to keep Uncle Nate waiting,' said Riley, hopping from one foot to the next.

Robert slung his arm around his friend's shoulder. 'Let's just have a quick look around first. See what's happening.'

Riley tried to be reassured by his friend's relaxed nature. 'Okay. But this

doesn't look like the badlands that we were driving through, does it?'

Robert surveyed the landscape. Riley was right. There were none of the rocky formations that were everywhere in the badlands of modern times. The boys could make out an internal sea, which Robert had read was called the Bearpaw Sea, off in the distance. And closer to them, the ground was swampy, with long matted reeds dotted around the edge of the swamps.

The boys had to tread carefully, and Robert led the way, looking out for

creatures with large teeth and murderous intent. He was heading towards a forested area when Riley yelped behind him.

'What is it?' asked Robert, alarmed. Riley practically jumped into his arms, pointing to a nearby swamp.

It looked as if the water was moving slowly. A moment later a large scaly head emerged, then ducked under again and drifted further away from the fascinated boys.

Robert pressed record on his voice recorder, a little breathless with excitement. 'I think Riley has just found our first prehistoric creature, and I reckon it's an *Archelon* (are-kell-on), a turtle that lived during the late Cretaceous period in North America.'

Riley took a closer look. 'That is one enormous turtle!'

Robert nodded. 'These guys can reach 3.6 metres in length — much bigger than any turtle humans have ever seen. And what's interesting is that they evolved to have a shell on their back. During the Cretaceous period, all they had was a tough leathery hide rather than a shell.'

Riley was impressed. 'This prehistoric stuff is much more interesting when you can actually see the creature you're talking about.'

'Let's keep moving,' said Robert. 'It's swampy around here, so be extra –'

There was a strange swallowing noise from behind Robert. He turned to see a speechless Riley disappearing from sight, as though the ground was swallowing him whole!

CHAPTER FOUR

'Get me out of here!' Riley managed to gasp, as he quickly sank to waist height in swampy sand.

'Okay, don't panic.' Robert spun around, looking for a vine or branch that he could use.

'Too late! Get me out of here!' Riley

grabbed helplessly at some reeds, but they slipped through his fingers.

Robert ran to a shrub that had woody vines draped all over it. With a sharp tug, he disentangled one and hurried back to his friend. 'Tie the end around your waist. Hurry!'

Riley wasted no time arguing. This was a matter of life or death. He wrapped the woody vine around his torso, and held tightly to the knot as Robert wound the other end round and round his left wrist, and started pulling slowly.

'It's working!' yelled Riley excitedly,

as he felt himself getting pulled from the sandy claws of the quicksand.

Robert wasn't about to mention this to Riley, but he was a little worried about making a lot of noise just in case it drew unwanted attention. He wasn't sure how well theropods could hear, but he figured the sound of a 9-year-old boy shouting his lungs out in the middle of a swamp could travel for miles.

Finally, with lots of effort by Robert and energetic yelling and wriggling by Riley, they got Riley out. He was a bit of a mess, and the humidity in the air meant that both boys were damp with sweat.

'Phew, that was a surprise,' said Robert, unravelling the woody vine from his arm and discarding it.

Riley was shaken. 'I was looking out for carnivores, not for quicksand.'

Robert helped dust his friend off. 'Let's head towards the forested area. Hopefully it'll be less swampy there. Follow in my footsteps.'

They walked carefully for a few hundred metres, and once they reached the forest's edge, the natural sunlight

was blocked, making everything a little darker and scarier.

Robert kept talking quietly to Riley, which helped to make them both feel less afraid. 'Apart from the turtles and other marine creatures, there are probably frogs and even small marsupials around here too. Keep your eyes peeled.'

Riley's eyes flickered from forest floor to treetops, taking it all in. 'I never thought I'd be saying this, but isn't it time we saw a dinosaur?'

Robert laughed. 'I was thinking the same thing, mate.'

A breathy whine floating through the trees interrupted the conversation.

Riley stopped. 'What was that?'

'I'm not sure.' Robert frowned.

They listened again. There was another whine.

'Let's go and investigate!' whispered Robert, his eyes sparkling with excitement, as they headed towards the mysterious noise.

CHAPTER FIVE

The whines turned into grunts as the
boys edged closer. Finally Robert and
Riley got close enough to see the source
of the unusual sound.

'Hey, look. Two army tanks,' whispered Riley.

There were two heavily plated

ankylosaurs at the base of a large redwood tree.

Robert was almost jumping up and down. 'They're *euoplocephaluses*, Riley. Incredible!' He grabbed his voice recorder once more. 'So we're in a deeply forested area and we've come across two *euoplocephaluses*. They're enormous, much bigger than I would've imagined, around 6 metres long, and one of them is using its duck-billed beak to chew on a shrub.'

Riley pointed to the second anklyosaur. 'What's up with that guy?'

42

Robert continued his commentary. 'The second *euoplocephalus*, who is slightly smaller than his friend, seems to have tried to eat a vine that has tangled up one of his legs . . .'

The creature let out another breathy whine, similar to the one the boys had heard earlier.

'. . . and he's not happy about it. He's trying to chew through the vine, but it looks like the same kind of vine I used to help Riley out of the quicksand. Poor guy. It's going to take him a while to cut through that.' Robert pocketed his voice recorder.

The *euoplocephalus* was making the knot around his front leg worse, and was becoming more agitated. His companion didn't stop to help out, and instead was concentrating solely on chomping his own shrub. Obviously, in this environment, food came before friends.

'I'm glad they're not meat-eaters, Robert – they look tough!' said Riley, impressed.

Robert punched his friend on the arm. 'Exactly what I've been trying to say all day, mate. These guys are protective powerhouses. Just because they don't

have the enormous jaws and teeth of the carnivore, doesn't mean they aren't awesome creatures.'

'Okay, well, I get what you were saying. Now I can see with my own eyes.' Riley shook his head. 'It is really amazing, isn't it?'

Robert smiled. 'I'm glad you're here to see it with me.'

All of a sudden, the larger *euoplocephalus* stopped eating, raised its head in the air and sniffed.

Riley looked worried. 'Do you think they can smell us?'

'I'm not sure.'

The smaller *euoplocephalus* was still busy fighting the vine.

After a second sniff, the free dinosaur started pawing the ground and let out a couple of snorts.

Meanwhile, the smaller *euoplocephalus* became more desperate, pawing and chewing the vine at the same time.

Robert was intrigued. 'This behaviour makes me think that the dinosaurs have sensed some kind of danger.'

Riley tensed. 'Then we should be getting away from here.'

'*Euoplocephaluses* have quite small brains, so it may be a false alarm.'

Riley looked at Robert incredulously. 'Mate, if there's a chance something with big teeth and an appetite is on its way here, I don't want to be the easy meal option.' He put on his carnivorous dinosaur voice. '"Hmmm, I could chew on a tough leathery dinosaur over there or go for the softer and tastier-looking human boy." Seriously, I'd know which meal I'd choose.'

Robert considered Riley's argument. 'Good point. Let's get off the ground.

But I want to keep an eye on this *euoplocephalus*, see if we can help him.'

As the boys found shelter, the larger *euoplocephalus* was now butting its buddy to get a move on.

The smaller 'saur was looking more and more frantic, but didn't seem to have the ability to untangle itself. Its companion sniffed the air once more and then took off, without a backwards glance, through a copse of trees.

The remaining *euoplocephalus* glanced after its departing friend, let out a whine and continued to struggle.

CHAPTER SIX

It only took a moment for the predator to arrive. Riley had to stifle a cry. It did not look like the type of dinosaur you wanted to get too close to. 'What is it?' asked Riley, not sure if he really wanted to know the answer.

Robert stared at the creature in

amazement. 'I think it's a *Gorgosaurus* (gorr-goh-saw-russ).'

Riley shook his head. 'That's *another* dinosaur I've never heard of before.'

'It's very similar to *albertosaurus*,' Robert explained. 'It's a carnivore, and as you can see, its head is really large compared to the rest of its body. Smaller than *Tyrannosaurus rex* but just as deadly!'

As if responding to Robert's cue, the *gorgosaurus* opened its mouth and gave a bloodcurdling roar as he focused in on the *euoplocephalus*.

The *euoplocephalus* was trapped. Its tail was thrashing from side to side, but the persistent vine was not releasing its grip.

Robert started climbing down the tree.

'What are you doing?' whisper-shouted Riley. 'Are you crazy?'

Robert looked up at his friend, who was perched on a branch. 'Stay there, okay? I'm going to try to create a distraction.'

Before Riley could stop him, Robert scampered down to ground level and disappeared from sight. Riley's attention turned back to the *gorgosaurus*. It was moving closer to the *euoplocephalus*, taking its time. There was no need to rush when dinner was tethered to a tree, waiting for you.

Riley couldn't bear to watch the armoured dinosaur get eaten. Even in the short time he'd seen him, he'd grown to like the tough creature.

In fact, Riley thought that if he were a dinosaur, he'd be like this guy. Sometimes, simple things like having a snack turned into unfortunate accidents for Riley too. He was just lucky he didn't

live in a time where an accident could involve getting eaten in one gulp by a hungry *gorgosaurus*.

With this realisation, Riley decided he wasn't going to stay in the tree either. He'd do what he could to help this dinosaur survive. Riley started climbing down the tree, but only a couple of branches down he lost his footing, falling the last couple of metres.

And in true Riley fashion – he couldn't help himself, after all – his *AAAARRRRGGGHHH* could be heard resounding throughout the Cretaceous period.

Robert was collecting large stones from a rocky area a few metres away from the drama when Riley's yell alerted him. His plan had been to throw as many rocks as possible into a nearby fern, hopefully attracting the attention of the *gorgosaurus* and giving the ankylosaur more time to break free. But he realised Riley's outburst might prove a more successful distraction . . . albeit a deadly one.

He kept a couple of the stones and

ran back to the tree where he'd left Riley behind. Riley was no longer there and neither was the *gorgosaurus*.

Oh no. Something had just gone very, very wrong!

CHAPTER SEVEN

'Ri-ley!' shouted Robert, trying desperately to track down his friend.

There was no answer.

The trapped *euoplocephalus* looked over at the human boy in amazement. The poor ankylosaur had no idea what was going on. He whinnied in confusion.

Robert was worried for his friend, but he also knew that Riley had nine lives. Considering the amount of times his friend had got himself into death-defying trouble, he'd always managed to get out alive.

In a snap decision, Robert jogged over to the *euoplocephalus*, avoiding the club tail, which had started swinging in agitation. 'G'day, mate, my name's Robert,' he said quietly and calmly to the dinosaur. 'You've got yourself in a bind. Let me help.'

Of course the ankylosaur didn't know

what Robert was saying, but the soothing tone got the message across. It's tail stopped swinging.

Robert knew this was dangerous. There were spikes all over this dinosaur that could seriously hurt him. He grabbed hold of the woody vine wrapped tightly around the *euoplocephalus's* leg and, as quickly as he could, began to unwind it.

He spoke as he worked. 'This vine is fantastic for helping a friend out of quicksand, but I'd stay away from it as a food source. Okay?'

Using one of the stones he'd kept with him, Robert managed to cut the twisted vine with repeated blows. He pulled the last of the vine away from the *euoplocephalus's* foot, and discovered the end had got caught behind one of the armoured plates on its neck.

Finally the dinosaur was able to lift its released leg and back away, but the vine that was still attached to its neck stopped it from going any further.

'Let me finish. I'll have you free in a moment.' Robert grabbed the vine and pulled hard, finally dislodging it. 'There.

I've done it. You're dismissed, soldier.' He watched as the *euoplocephalus* moved its neck, sniffed the air, turned and then ran down the track into the forest.

Robert looked around him. The ferns rustled quietly in the gentle breeze. If it weren't for his friend having disappeared into thin air alongside a carnivorous dinosaur, he would have enjoyed the peaceful scene a lot more.

'Ri-ley!' Robert called out.

All of a sudden he could hear some-one, or something, running through the forest. But the acoustics were strange,

and he couldn't tell which direction the sound was coming from.

From the bush behind him came an explosion. Riley appeared, red-faced and wide-eyed. 'Run, mate, run!'

CHAPTER EIGHT

Robert didn't need to be told twice. He ran, and from the snorting, huffing sound behind him, realised that the hungry *gorgosaurus* was in hot pursuit! He wasn't sure how long the carnivore had been chasing Riley, but he was impressed his friend had survived this long!

The boys got whipped in the face with fern fronds and the odd vine as they sprinted through the forest, but they didn't waste precious breath complaining about it. They dodged rocks, stones, branches and a couple of unnamed large rodents, which promptly scattered when they saw what was after the boys.

'What made you think outrunning a *gorgosaurus* was a good idea?' asked Robert, as they jumped over a small stream.

Riley wheezed before replying, 'I didn't want to see the armoured tank go down.'

Robert grinned at his friend. 'I got him loose in the end. You probably saved his life, you know.'

'You can call me Riley Harper, Dinosaur Rescuer, from now on,' puffed Riley, and the duo ducked around another ferny area.

'I'll be calling you Riley Harper, Dinosaur *Food,* if we don't get this *gorgosaurus* off our tail soon!' quipped Robert.

The *gorgosaurus* steadfastly refused to give up. It had walked away from an easy dinner, and was not going to stop running until it tried this unusual species ahead. There was a bonus too. If the first one tasted good, there were seconds not far behind!

After sidestepping around a particularly large tree trunk, the boys screeched to a stop near the edge of a rocky outcrop.

Whoooaa!

Below them was a sheer drop of at least 15 metres. There was nowhere else to run.

The boys turned around to see the *gorgosaurus* also grind to a halt, wearing a victor's large-toothed smile.

Robert turned to Riley. He was puffing so hard he had trouble speaking. 'Riley, mate, sorry about this.'

Riley was gulping in breaths. 'Would be good to have some . . . great defensive tactic to use right now.'

Robert sighed. 'Copy that, soldier.'

At that moment thunder struck, which was surprising because it was a nice sunny day without a cloud to be seen. Confused, the *gorgosaurus* and the boys looked up at the sky.

CHAPTER NINE

The two boys glanced at each other, then at the sky again, then at the gorgosaurus, who seemed just as confused as the boys.

All of a sudden the thundering got closer, and four tank-like *euoplocephaluses*, trampling over ferns and other shrubs, appeared at the forest's

edge. They stopped in one defensive line, heads down, spikes gleaming, as though they were answering the call of an army general.

Robert noted that the smaller 'saur on the edge of the line was the one he'd rescued earlier. He allowed himself a grin. 'I think our backup troops have arrived.'

Riley's eyes were as big as saucers. 'How is this going to play out?'

Robert shrugged. 'Let's wait and see.' He looked behind him, down at the 15-metre drop. 'We have nowhere else to go.'

The *gorgosaurus* was also considering its options. It could take on a smaller
euoplocephalus tangled up in a vine, but
four creatures, appearing as though they
were ready for serious action, were a
force to be reckoned with.

The *gorgosaurus* let out an angry
roar. But the *euoplocephaluses* stood
their ground, refusing to budge.

The *gorgosaurus* roared once more,
in a 'this is just not my lucky day' sort
of way, and daintily moved to the edge
of the line of ankylosaurs before bolting
back into the forest.

Riley and Robert started clapping and cheering. 'Awesome work, guys!'

The *euoplocephaluses* lifted their heads, turned around and trundled back into the forest.

Robert and Riley saluted as the dinosaurs retreated.

'Enough adventure for today?' asked Robert with a tired grin.

'Well, I'm growing to like the place, but unless we can get a vegemite sandwich around here,' joked Riley, 'we have to go back.'

Robert considered the possibility.

'I'm not sure what year vegemite was invented, but I think it probably wasn't 70 million years ago.'

Riley nodded seriously. 'Probably not.' He glanced around. 'So how do we leave this place?'

'I think we need water,' said Robert. 'Let's head back to that swampy area across the forest.'

'Copy that, soldier,' said Riley, and the two boys strode off, marching in formation.

CHAPTER TEN

The two friends had an uneventful trip back through the forest.

While Robert used the time to record what had happened between the *gorgosaurus* and the *euoplocephaluses*, Riley tried to avoid falling into more quicksand or getting chased by a carnivore.

He did narrowly miss getting bitten by what looked like a prehistoric mosquito, though it wasn't the size of a modern-day mozzie. It was about a hundred times bigger. Riley used a fern frond to bat the creature out of his path and watched it hit a nearby tree trunk with a satisfying thud.

Normally this would've been big news, but after what had already happened today, a prehistoric, monster-sized mozzie was not even worth mentioning.

When the boys finally reached the swamp, Robert got out the fossil and

the two friends splashed water on each other . . . and nothing happened.

Robert sighed. 'I think we might have to jump in.'

Riley did a quick check to make sure the swamp wasn't harbouring any archelon or plesiosaurs, and announced, 'Last one in's a rotten egg!' Then he grabbed his friend and together they dive-bombed into the water.

Robert and Riley felt intensely wet, then dizzy, then wet again, and then as though they were falling through a tornado during a storm.

Arriving back by their tranquil camp site moments later, the boys were sprawled in a wet heap. Robert felt the compact weight of the digital voice recorder in his pocket as he got up. 'Good thing it's waterproof,' he thought.

Uncle Nate reappeared with two bottles of drinking water, and gave the boys a curious once-over. 'Okay then. You decided to swim in the lake . . . with your clothes on.' He shrugged. 'Why not?' He handed the two boys a bottle of water each. 'Cheers.'

Later that evening, Uncle Nate and the two boys were sleeping peacefully. The sound of a great horned owl could be heard in the distance.

Ho hoo hoo hoododo. Ho hoo hoo hoododo.

Suddenly Riley sat bolt upright, arms flailing, screaming, 'Get the *gorgosaurus* off me!'

Uncle Nate and Robert jerked awake, startled by the outburst.

'What did you say, little guy?' asked a bleary-eyed Uncle Nate.

Riley looked around, realising he'd been dreaming. 'Oh, ummm, nothing.'

Uncle Nate glanced over at him. 'You were dreaming of being eaten by a what? A *gorgosaurus*?'

Riley was a little embarrassed. 'Sort of.'

Robert came to his friend's rescue. 'That's strange, because I'd been dreaming about an *albertosaurus* climbing into the station wagon while we were stopped at traffic lights.'

Uncle Nate seemed bewildered. 'You boys have extremely imaginative

dreams. But I guess that as long as your waking life isn't dangerous, there's no harm done.' He lay back on his pillow and was snoring softly seconds later.

Riley and Robert shared a look.

'Sleep well, mate,' yawned Robert.

Riley grinned. 'Don't let the bedbugs bite.'

Robert looked serious. 'It's actually the scorpions you have to be careful of around here.'

Riley jerked back upright, eyes wide in alarm, as Robert snuggled into his sleeping bag, chuckling to himself.

Drawn by Robert Irwin

EUOPLOCEPHALUS

ALSO KNOWN AS: Dyoplosaurus

DISCOVERED: 1902 in Alberta, Canada

ETYMOLOGY: Well-armoured head

PERIOD: Late Cretaceous period, 70–65
million years ago

LENGTH: Approtimately 6 metres long

HEIGHT: Approtimately 1.8 metres tall

WEIGHT: Approtimately 2 tonnes

Euoplocephaluses were herbivores
that thrived towards the end of
the Cretaceous period. They

were built like military tanks, and some species were about the same size. Massive hips and legs supported their heavy bodies. They had thick plates and spikes on their backs, but the armour on their heads was much more developed. They also had a unique weapon — a large ball of bone at the end of their tail, which could be swung from side to side like a club.

Euoplocephalus's head was a heavy bot of bone, covered in thick plates. Thick spines protected the sides of its face, and even its eyelids were armoured.

There was a horny, toothless beak at the front of its wide face.

Euoplocephalus was discovered in 1902

by Lawrence Lambe, who proposed the name 'stereocephalus'. However, this term was already being used for an insect, so the name of the dinosaur was changed to *euoplocephalus* in 1910.

Two species of *euoplocephaluses* are known to have existed: the original species, *Euoplocephalus tutus*, and a second species, *Euoplocephalus acutosquameus*, which was discovered in 1924 by William Arthur Parks. The species have different shaped clubs in their tails, but despite this, some scientists believe they are in fact a single species.

Euoplocephalus is the best-known ankylosaur among paleontologists, with the discovery of over 40 more-or-less complete skeletons (including about 15 intact skulls). However, since the remains of multiple *euoplocephaluses* have never been found heaped together, it's likely that this herbivore led a solitary lifestyle, though some experts believe *euoplocephalus* may have roamed the North American plains in small herds.

THE CANADIAN BADLANDS

This region in Alberta, Canada is famous for rich deposits of fossils, including dinosaur bones, which can be seen at the UNESCO World Heritage Site Dinosaur Provincial Park, and are displayed at the Royal Tyrrell Museum.

Dinosaur Provincial Park is located in the heart of the province of Alberta's badlands and contains some of the most important fossil discoveries ever made from the Age of Reptiles, in particular about 35 species of dinosaur that date back 75 million years.

More than 300 dinosaur skeletons have been pulled from a 27-kilometre stretch along the Red Deer River since digging began there in the 1880s, and dozens of these now grace museums in 30 cities around the world. Since 1985 the largest collection of treasures from the park has been housed in the Royal Tyrrell Museum of Palaeontology in Drumheller, Canada.

Interested in finding out what Robert does when he's not hunting for dinosaurs?

Check out www.australiazoo.com.au

Loved the book?

There's so much more
stuff to check out online

AUSTRALIAN READERS:

randomhouse.com.au/kids

NEW ZEALAND READERS:

randomhouse.co.nz/kids